PHYLLIS S. BUSCH

THE
SEVEN SLEEPERS

THE STORY OF HIBERNATION

**ILLUSTRATED BY
WAYNE TRIMM**

MACMILLAN PUBLISHING COMPANY / New York
COLLIER MACMILLAN PUBLISHERS / London

To Big Ben,
grandfather of
Little Ben

Macmillan books are available at special discounts
for bulk purchases for sales promotions, premiums,
fund-raising, or educational use. Special editions
or book excerpts can also be created to specifications.
For details, contact:
Special Sales Director
Macmillan Publishing Company
866 Third Avenue
New York, N.Y. 10022

Macmillan Publishing Company
866 Third Avenue, New York, N.Y. 10022
Collier Macmillan Canada, Inc.
Printed in the United States of America
10 9 8 7 6 5 4 3 2 1
Library of Congress Cataloging in Publication Data
Busch, Phyllis S.
The seven sleepers.
Summary: Discusses how and why animals hibernate and
how they survive during their long winter sleep.
Also considers the application of hibernation techniques
to human beings.
1. Hibernation—Juvenile literature. [1. Hibernation]
I. Trimm, H. Wayne, ill. II. Title.
QL755.B89   1985   591.54'3   84-42984
ISBN 0-02-715650-8

The BAT and the BEAR they never care
What winter winds may blow,
The JUMPING MOUSE in his cozy house
Is safe from ice and snow;
The CHIPMUNK and the WOODCHUCK,
The SKUNK who's slow but sure,
The ringed RACCOON who hates the moon
Have found for cold the cure.

—Ernest Thompson Seton

◆ CONTENTS ◆

WINTER

Where do all the shivering animals go
When the cold wintry winds from up north do blow?
The Squirrels, the Chipmunks, the Robins, the Bees,
The Woodchuck, the Rabbits, the gay Chickadees?

Do all the animals go away for the winter? Some of them leave, but they return. These travelers are called migrators. They go south in the autumn and come back in the spring. This round-trip journey is a migration.

Many animals do not leave. They remain where they are and continue to be active all winter. You can find these animals if you know where to look for them.

The third group of animals is the most interesting. Even though they do not go away, they are hard to find during the cold weather. These animals go into a deep sleep before it turns cold and remain asleep for all or part of the winter. Most of these sleepers take their long winter naps underground.

Many animals live in places where winters are harsh. They have to protect themselves from the cold in order to survive. Each kind of animal does this in a different way.

Why is winter so cold in some places, and why do

animals need special protection at this time?

The circle of the seasons goes round and round, year after year. The winter season follows autumn. Autumn comes after summer. Summer arrives after spring. Then spring catches up with winter once more.

The earth makes a complete turn, or rotation, once each day. The earth's turning gives us a night and a day every twenty-four hours. When our part of the world turns toward the sun, it is daytime. When it turns away from the sun, it is night.

The earth has another movement. At the same time that it is spinning, it also travels around the sun. It takes the earth a little more than a year to complete a single trip around the sun. A round trip lasts 365¼ days.

The seasons change because the spinning earth travels around the sun and because the earth is tilted. The weather is different in each season. These differences are greatest in those parts of the world known as the Temperate Zones. Most of the earth's people live in these zones.

As spring goes into summer, our part of the earth slants toward the sun. Days get longer, and the sun is more directly overhead. Direct sunrays give off much heat. In addition, there is more time for the earth to warm up when the days are longer.

Summertime is a warm, sunny time. Plants make food and grow. Animals also grow as they feed on plants or on plant eaters. However, summertime does not last forever.

The slanting, spinning earth continues to move. As it moves, our part of the world begins to tilt away from the sun. The sun's rays are no longer overhead, so they give off less heat. The days get shorter. The weather becomes chilly. Soon the warm summer is over. Cooler autumn follows. Then comes the cold, harsh winter.

December, January, and February are the coldest months north of the equator. December has the shortest days. It is dark at bedtime, and it is still dark when it is time to get up. There are few daylight hours.

Northern winters are often cold and dreary. There are no blooming flowers. There are no bees, butterflies, or other insects. There are few trees with bright green leaves. Some seeds and dried fruits remain, but, generally, food for animals is scarce. And snow may cover the ground.

ANIMALS THAT MIGRATE

Some animals go south before winter arrives. They travel to places that are warmer, where they can also find a good supply of food. After the northern winter, spring returns. So do the animals. It is warm once more and there is enough food for them. The migrators have skipped winter entirely.

Many kinds of animals migrate. Birds are among the most spectacular migrators. During spring and summer they are busy feeding and raising families. Some of these are familiar birds such as robins, wrens, bluebirds, swallows, warblers, and hawks. They fly about, sing, build nests, and care for their babies. They find plenty of food such as insects, berries, or earthworms.

Toward the end of summer, birds begin to gather in flocks. Flocks of swallows often perch along telephone lines, and robins may gather in trees. One day the swallows are gone. Soon the robins leave. Gradually all the migrators have started on their journey south.

The robins may be flying to a place in Central America that is about four thousand miles (six thousand kilometers) away. Bobolinks may travel even more. Some spend the winter in Argentina, a country in South America almost six thousand miles (ten thousand kilometers) away.

For some reason a few of these birds may not migrate. They remain behind and huddle together in some protected spot all winter. They feed on the remaining dried seeds and berries. They may pick on a lump of suet that someone has fastened to a tree. Many dine at bird feeders.

Some birds migrate north of the United States, all the way to the Arctic to breed. When nesting time is over they migrate south. Many of these birds spend the winter in the United States. Among them are juncos, tree sparrows, and evening grosbeaks. The best way to see these attractive birds is to provide them with food. They always go to feeders that have a constant supply of sunflower seeds. Birds need a great deal of nourishment in the winter in order to keep warm.

Snowy owls are some of the most attractive visitors from the north. These beautiful white birds usually spend their winters in Canada. They feed chiefly on lemmings, small animals that are related to mice and rats. When there is a shortage of lemmings, snowy owls come south to the United States, searching for food.

Several kinds of bats live in the United States. They feed on flying insects. These insects disappear in the winter, so most bats migrate south, where there is a good insect supply. By the time mosquitoes begin to annoy us once more, the bats have returned.

There are large animal migrators as well as small ones. Herds of moose and elk spend their summers in the highlands. When it turns very cold in November, they return to the lowlands, the valleys.

Reindeer and caribou are animals of the north. They

depend on low-growing plants for food. When snow begins to fall, it covers these plants, so the reindeer and caribou migrate from Arctic areas to southern lands.

Among the smallest animals to migrate are the monarch butterflies. Hundreds of thousands of these beautiful orange and black creatures fly south each year. There are special places where they all gather. The western monarchs collect in California, and the eastern monarchs travel all the way to a certain mountain in Mexico. The butterflies spend an inactive winter, clinging to the leaves and twigs of trees.

When spring arrives, the insects mate and start on their northward journey. Not many make it all the way home. The females stop to lay their eggs, one at a time, as they migrate north. These eggs hatch into a generation of monarchs that do not migrate. They live only about one month. However, these nonmigrating monarchs produce butterflies that live about ten months, and this generation is the migrating monarch.

Some water animals, as well as land animals, migrate. For example, tunas, herrings, and smelts are migrating fishes.

All of these and many more kinds of animals have an instinct for such travels. They have to migrate in order to survive.

ANIMALS THAT REMAIN ACTIVE ALL WINTER

Many animals do not migrate when winter comes, but remain in the same general area all year long. During the warm summer days, there is plenty of food, and life seems easy. Cold weather is much harder for most of them. This is especially true for warm-blooded animals such as birds, mice, squirrels, and people. They have a warm body temperature that remains the same. If their temperature drops too low, they get a chill. If it rises too high, they suffer from a fever.

Warm-blooded animals need food and protection all winter long in order to survive. Each kind prepares for winter in a different way. This is not a decision the animal makes, for each is designed by nature to behave in a certain way that is best for its survival.

A familiar example is the gray squirrel. These warm-blooded animals are always busy, but they become even busier in the autumn. They scurry up and down trees, collecting acorns and other nuts. The squirrels may stop to eat some, but they bury most of them. Week after week, they make many collecting trips. The squirrels dig separate little holes in which to bury each nut.

When winter comes, the gray squirrels are just as busy digging them up again. No matter how thick the snow, the squirrels plunge down and burrow for their food. One wonders how they know where to look. Some scientists think that squirrels can smell acorns.

One squirrel eats about forty pounds (eighteen kilograms) of acorns in a single winter. Acorns are an important winter food for many other kinds of wildlife as well. Chipmunks, deer, and wild turkeys are some other animals that feed on them.

Not all acorns are eaten, however. Many of them are never found. They remain buried. Some of these sprout and grow into little oak trees. Small oaks grow into big ones. Finally they are old enough to produce a new crop of acorns. In this way the forests continue to grow trees, and many wild animals continue to have food for winter.

The gray squirrel is not only provided with a winter food supply. It also gets a warmer coat for the cold weather. A solid gray, thicker fur coat takes the place of the thinner, brown and gray summer one. Its bushy tail becomes even bushier. When the gray squirrel takes a nap, it keeps warm by wrapping its tail around its face.

Gray squirrels pile stacks of dry leaves high up among some tree branches. Their winter nests may look messy but they are warm and safe. Later in the year, the gray squirrel babies will find protection in these nests.

Red squirrels also frisk about during the winter. Their fur changes to a richer red on the back. Little tufts of white fur appear on their ears, which may also add some warmth. Red squirrels feed chiefly on seeds from the cones of evergreen trees. They hide many of these in a tree hollow or under some leaves on the ground. Sometimes they store mushrooms along with the tree seeds. Now and then a gray squirrel meets a red squirrel trying to get the same hidden food. This causes a noisy squabble. Finally, one of them leaves.

When the weather is very bad, the red squirrels become less active. They may retire to their nests in hollow trees or stumps for a day or more at a time.

Another animal that remains active all winter is the deer. Its tracks are often seen in the snow. Deer move about a great deal as they search for food and water. These animals can stand the cold and snow because their fur coats are thicker and tougher in the winter. The thin, reddish summer fur is replaced by a denser, gray fur. Longer, curly hairs grow in. These hairs trap a layer of air next to the body, which insulates the deer. The insulation prevents the heat from escaping the deer's body.

Deer are plant eaters. They browse mostly on the twigs of shrubs and on the bottom branches of trees. Sometimes there are too many deer wintering in one place. A heavy snowfall can cover their food supply and cause many deer to starve.

The red fox can also be seen in winter. This slender animal looks much larger at this time of year because it grows extra fur. Under its regular fur, an additional furry layer develops. Its tail also becomes much bushier. When the fox sleeps, it keeps warm by wrapping its tail over its face and paws.

Some animals survive more easily in the winter because the color of their fur changes to white.

The snowshoe rabbit is one such animal. It is grayish

brown in summer. Toward the end of the season, brown hairs with white tips grow in among the all-brown ones. This animal, which is so brown in summer, gradually becomes very white in winter. This makes it hard for its enemies to find it in the snow.

The brown short-tailed weasel also turns white in winter. Only the tip of its tail is black. It is a small animal. When it runs across the snow, all that can be seen easily is a jumping black dot.

Mice and moles remain active under the snow all through the cold weather. There are large numbers of these animals. They keep warm under the snow blanket and find protection there. They are small, but they need a great deal of food to survive the winter. The meadow mice feed on grasses and bark. The moles dig for worms or for any insect food that may be in the ground.

Deer mice make a different kind of cozy winter home. They use old bird nests in trees. They add some shredded leaves and bark to make a soft bed. Then they put a roof over the top of the nest. Home is complete after a supply of nuts is stored there for winter use. A knock on the tree often arouses the animal from a winter nap. A little brown head with two large eyes appears at the edge of the nest. It seems to inquire who the visitor might be.

Many deer mice spend their winters indoors. They may select a drawer or a shoe in which to nest. It is not unusual to open a dresser drawer in a farmhouse and find a whole family of deer mice all softly bedded down on a shredded tablecloth or quilt.

Many nonmigrating birds live in the north all year as permanent residents. People who like to see birds attract them by providing them with food all winter. Some resident birds are crows, bluejays, cardinals, chickadees, nuthatches, and woodpeckers.

Other interesting birds to be seen at bird feeders are known as the winter visitors. These breed far to the north and spend their winters in the northern United States. Among these visitors are evening grosbeaks, juncos, and tree sparrows. The squirrels often join the bird parties.

Birds keep warm in winter by growing an extra layer of fat. Feathers also help to keep them warm by insulating their bodies with a layer of air next to the skin. Birds can fluff up their feathers until they look twice their normal size. When the feathers stand up, they trap the air.

The ruffed grouse (which some people call a partridge) is often seen in the winter. At this time of year it grows extensions on its toes that act like snowshoes. They make it easier for the grouse to walk over the snow. In big storms, the grouse sometimes jumps headfirst into a snowbank. It's warmer under the snow, and the grouse remains there until the storm passes.

Insects are not around only in the summertime. Quite a few can be found in the winter, even on the snow.

Near a swift-running brook, you might see crane flies. Winter is their breeding time. They come out of the soil through the snow to seek mates. They have long legs and no wings. After mating, they return to the soil to lay their eggs.

Among the commonest winter insects are snow fleas. These wingless creatures are also known as springtails, for they have a tail that acts like a spring. They can jump a distance of several centimeters.

Springtails live in damp earth and feed on dead plants. On a sunny day in February or March, you may see tiny black specks moving on the snow. These are thousands and thousands of snow fleas marching in search of food.

One thinks of bees as insects that fly among the flowers on hot summer days. But bees remain active all year. During the cold weather, they spend most of their time in the hive. They work to keep the hive clean and warm. They also take care of the queen bee, who will lay many eggs the following spring.

During the winter, the bees have to keep eating. They make short trips outdoors to get rid of their wastes. Bees sometimes wander too far from the hive and get too cold to return. They fall on the snow as if they were dead, but most are just numb. It is best not to pick them up unless one knows how to handle bees. Some can be revived if they are warmed for a short time. Then they are ready to go back into the hive.

Cold, icy waters also have animals that remain active all winter. Shallow little pools of water may have a crust of ice on top. Even before the ice melts, one can see the fairy shrimp and water fleas. These waters may dry up in the spring because most shallow pools are temporary. However, there is much activity in them near the end of winter.

Fairy shrimp are about an inch long. They mate quickly and lay eggs that can survive for an entire year.

Water fleas, also known as daphnia, are not insects. Daphnia are flat, transparent little animals much smaller than fairy shrimp. Their insides can be seen when they are observed through a microscope. The females carry their eggs in a special little bag on their back.

Some large water animals also remain active in ponds and lakes. Even when there is a thick cover of ice on top of the water, down below you can find salamanders, such as the spotted newts. Salamanders feed on water insects.

You can find yellow perch, which go after smaller fish as well as insects. The northern pike is also active in such cold waters. Where there are fish, there are fishermen. Ice fishing is a popular winter sport.

Humans also remain active all year. Those who live in areas where there are cold winters can survive the cold because they know how to keep warm. They heat and insulate their buildings. They wear clothing that is warm and waterproof. They grow and store enough food for the winter.

People learned how to survive by using their brains. They imitated animals in some ways and invented still other ways to survive. This is why people can live and work in almost any part of the world. They can also teach other people what they learn.

Other animals cannot think up new ways for surviving cold winters. Neither can they teach much of this to their young. Each inherits the instincts for the right kind of behavior. Their bodies have to be warmed, and they must know how to protect themselves. They also need to do the right things about getting food in winter. All this comes naturally to those that survive.

HIBERNATION

Some animals do not migrate in order to survive the cold. Neither do they remain active all year. This third group hibernates. This means that the animals take a very long winter nap. They may remain fast asleep for several months. There are hibernators that go to sleep before summer and sleep through summer, autumn, and winter. They do not awaken until spring arrives. Some of these animals spend more time sleeping than being awake. Most of them, however, hibernate for three or four months. They are asleep during that part of the year when it is very cold and food is scarce.

When an animal goes into hibernation, everything that keeps it alive either stops or slows down. The heart beats more slowly, and, therefore, the blood moves through the body at a much slower rate. The animal barely breathes. While it is in a deep sleep, it does not eat. Neither does it get rid of its wastes. The body temperature drops way down. The animal becomes very cold, just a few degrees above freezing. It usually conserves heat by rolling itself into a ball. It remains that way until it comes out of hibernation.

While the animal is hibernating, it looks and acts more

dead than alive. But it is not dead. In fact, it is very much alive.

Sometimes the air that surrounds a hibernator drops down to freezing. The animal cannot live if it remains at such a low temperature. However, the brain of a hibernator immediately sends out body signals to save it. The animal starts shivering. This movement warms the body. Its stored body fat provides more heat at once. The animal warms up a bit and remains alive.

The Ground Squirrel

Although a great deal is known about hibernation, much remains to be discovered. Scientists have been studying the ground squirrel for many years in order to learn more about the process of hibernation because these animals spend much of their lives hibernating. They resemble chipmunks without any face stripes. When ground squirrels are not hibernating they make their homes in underground burrows. The ground squirrels satisfy their enormous appetites with all kinds of wild plants. The midwestern and western parts of North America are home to many kinds of ground squirrels.

These animals disappear completely toward the end of summer. They are not seen again until the following spring, when woodsmen often see them come right out of the earth and shake themselves free of the soil. Some of these people did not believe that animals could remain alive in soil that had been frozen solid. They insisted that the ground squirrels died and remained buried all winter and then came alive again in the spring. This was before anything was known about hibernation. Of course this is untrue, but some people still believe it.

The ground squirrels start to prepare for hibernation in late summer. They receive a signal from the brain to start eating. They eat and eat and eat. There is plenty of food for plant eaters at this time.

If there should be a food shortage one year, the animals hibernate earlier. However, they must grow a certain amount of fat on their bodies before hibernating. If they are too thin, they do not hibernate.

In addition to eating a great deal, the ground squirrels prepare their winter quarters. Each squirrel takes its long nap in an underground burrow on a soft bed of leaves and grasses.

These animals do not hibernate all at once. They go to sleep little by little. Each night, as the ground squirrel goes to sleep, its heart and lungs work more slowly. Its body temperature drops a few degrees. When its temperature is almost down to freezing, the animal is ready for its long winter sleep. It goes into hibernation. It may remain asleep for six to eight months.

Hibernation is very different from regular sleeping. When an animal takes its usual nap, it relaxes its body a little and falls asleep for a few hours only. There is a slight drop in its body temperature while it is asleep. During hibernation the body is completely relaxed, and there is a big drop in body temperature. In addition, hibernation sleep lasts for months.

Throughout hibernation, the ground squirrel remains

rolled up. It tucks in its paws and places its tail over its head. In this round shape, its body loses the least amount of heat.

A person's hand also keeps warmer when it is rolled up. Try this. Make a fist with your left hand. Keep the right open. Hold these positions for one minute. Open your fist and immediately place the palms of both hands on your cheeks. The hand that was rolled up feels warmer because it lost less body heat. The open hand lost more heat; therefore, it feels cooler.

If the ground squirrel is disturbed during hibernation, it may awaken with a shriek. Its body temperature can become normal in about three hours. However, it can go back into hibernation when no longer disturbed.

The ground squirrel knows when to start its long nap. It also knows, as though an alarm had gone off inside it, that springtime is waking-up time.

A part of the ground squirrel's brain acts like a body clock. It signals the time when certain parts of the body must carry out special jobs. These jobs, or functions, must be carried out in order to keep the squirrel alive. These jobs include eating, sleeping, hibernating, and awakening from hibernation.

The ground squirrel comes out of hibernation faster than it goes into it. First its heart begins to beat quickly. The rapid heartbeat makes the blood circulate faster. Then the squirrel begins to breathe more rapidly, and its body temperature rises. Its brain, heart, and lungs warm up first, and then the rest of the body gets warmer. In a few hours the squirrel has revived completely.

The males are the first to come out of their burrows.

They have an urge to mate, so they begin to search other burrows, looking for a female. Mating soon takes place. A few weeks later the babies are born. They eat, grow, and do what ground squirrels do. When the young are old enough, they dig their own burrows.

Toward the end of the summer, the squirrels' brains send out signals that hibernating time is coming. They start to eat, and each ground squirrel repeats the same yearly cycle. They are born knowing what to do and when to do it.

Scientists have tried to fool some ground squirrels. In one experiment they kept them in a room that had a summer temperature all year long. They also gave the animals plenty of food. In spite of these conditions, the squirrels started to hibernate at the right time. Their body clocks sent out the same hibernating signals they would have sent if the animals had been living outdoors.

Some conditions do affect the ground squirrels' hibernating behavior. If they should be placed in a very cold room, they would go into hibernation even if it were July. Hibernation would also take place if they were kept in the dark or left without food. In this way, hibernation makes it possible for the ground squirrel to survive unfavorable conditions.

Experiments such as these are being carried on in the laboratories of Dr. Charles P. Lyman of the Harvard Medical School in Boston.

The Dormouse

The dormouse is a squirrellike European hibernator. It is active by night and sleeps all day. It hibernates for many months of the year. People always think of the dormouse as a sleepyhead, and this is how it got its name. It comes from the French verb *dormir*, which means "to sleep."

A sleeping dormouse is a popular character in a famous chapter of Lewis Carroll's book *Alice's Adventures in Wonderland*. In this chapter, called "A Mad Tea-Party," Alice wanders into a garden where a dormouse is seated at a tea table. The dormouse is fast asleep. On one side of him is the March Hare. The Mad Hatter sits on the other side. The March Hare and the Mad Hatter are talking to each other over the head of the sleeping dormouse. They keep trying to awaken it, but have no luck.

First, they pour hot water on its nose. It awakens with a shriek, but falls asleep again. Then they pinch it. This time it just blinks its eyes, shakes its head, and goes right on sleeping.

Alice thinks that it is a stupid party, and she decides to

leave. When she reaches the end of the garden, she looks back. There she sees the Mad Hatter and the March Hare trying to awaken the dormouse once more. This time they are shoving it into the teapot. No one knows what happens then.

A real dormouse does not drink tea, of course. Neither is it likely to go to parties. It feeds on plants and drinks water. It eats a great deal at the end of summer and becomes enormously fat. By October or early November, it is ready to hibernate. Its body temperature drops and its body works more and more slowly. The dormouse rolls into a ball and wraps its tail over its head and back. As its body temperature falls, it gets colder and stiffer.

If a scientist should place a hibernating dormouse on a table in a very cold room, it would just lie there. It can be rolled about like a fur ball without waking up. If the animal were pinched, however, it would awaken with a shriek, and it would go right back to sleep, as it did in *Alice's Adventures in Wonderland*. It would behave the same if it were awakened by pouring hot water on it. This would have to be done slowly, for it would die if it were awakened too quickly or with too much heat.

The dormouse, as well as other hibernating animals, starts to lose weight as soon as it goes into hibernation. No hibernating animals eat while asleep, but they do need energy in order to stay alive. They also need energy to warm up their cold bodies when they awaken. They get this energy from the fat they accumulated at the end of summer, which was stored as a thick layer under the skin. A dormouse that weighs 4 ounces (113 grams) in spring may weigh twice as much when it is ready to hibernate.

In another experiment on hibernation, scientists wanted to find out how quickly a hibernating animal loses weight. They put some dormice into a very cold room, and the animals soon went into hibernation.

The hibernating dormice were picked up and weighed regularly. Whenever they were weighed, they would awaken. Then they would go back to sleep. However, a dormouse uses a great deal of energy to get through the waking-up process. Since this energy comes from its stored fat, the animals became thinner and thinner as the experiment went on. After a few weeks, they did not go back into hibernation after being weighed. Their brains did not signal them to hibernate because they did not have enough fat left on their bodies. The amount of fat needed for hibernation is different for each kind of animal.

The Indians called hibernation the "long sleep." This long sleep is not only done by some warm-blooded animals such as ground squirrels and dormice. Many cold-blooded animals also hibernate. These animals find protection in places where the temperature will remain above freezing all winter. Some bury themselves in soil or mud underground. Some animals go under a pile of leaves. Others use caves. Still others crawl under the loose bark of trees.

Earthworms

 Earthworms hibernate in bunches underground. Sometimes several hundred mass together and form a ball of earthworms down in the soil below the frost line. Earthworms have no lungs. They breathe through their moist skins. When many of them hibernate together, they conserve moisture as well as heat.

Slugs

Slugs are related to snails, but have no shells. When these soft-bodied animals prepare for hibernation, they give off a slimy material. They spread this sticky slime over their bodies. It probably keeps them from drying out while underground. Each slug hibernates by itself.

Snails

Snails also hibernate. They crawl under a log or under a stone. Snails close their shells tightly with a cementlike material that comes from their bodies. Sometimes this lime spreads over several snails that lie in one place and they all become cemented together.

The Woolly Bear Caterpillar

 The woolly bear is possibly the only insect that hibernates while it is a caterpillar. When the weather gets cold, the fuzzy black and brown creature crawls under a rock or a doormat. It may even spend the winter rolled up in an old sneaker or in an empty carton. When spring returns, it completes its life cycle. It spins a brown cocoon and changes into a moth. The yellow adult is known as the Isabella tiger moth.

Ladybird Beetles

 Also called ladybugs, these insects hibernate as adults. They crawl under logs or seek protection behind some loose tree bark. Thousands may cluster in one spot. Many birds look for ladybird beetles as a source of winter food.

The Mourning Cloak Butterfly

Very few butterflies are known to hibernate as adults. The mourning cloak is one that does. It is a fairly large brown butterfly with a cream-colored edge on its wings. It is sometimes seen flying over patches of snow on a sunny day in late winter or very early in the spring. Another butterfly that hibernates as an adult is a smaller beauty known as the common blue or spring azure. These two butterflies spend the winter under the bark of trees. They fly out early in the season to find a place where they can lay their eggs.

Salamanders, Frogs, and Toads

Salamanders, frogs, and toads are also cold-blooded hibernators.

Spring peepers do not go very far down to hibernate. They may spend the winter at the edge of a pond under some frozen leaves. Their call is like that of a bird and a very welcome sound of early spring. If the air temperature rises to 50°F (10°C), their *peep-peep* can be heard. If the temperature falls, they become silent. As soon as it rises again, the peepers are heard once more. They sing in order to attract mates.

Toads usually hibernate by burying themselves in the mud. Frogs dig themselves into the muddy bottoms of ponds. They eat a great deal all summer and even more in the autumn. Then, before the soil freezes, they dig holes and bury themselves. While frogs are hibernating, they do not use their lungs to take in air. They breathe through their skins instead.

It is interesting to demonstrate how a frog goes into hibernation. The kind of common frog known as a meadow frog is a good one to use. Place the frog in a large jar containing cold water. The water should be about 2 inches (5 centimeters) deep. Fasten a piece of cheesecloth or screening over the top. This will allow air to enter the jar and prevent the frog from jumping out. A thermometer can also be placed inside the jar in order to read the temperature of the water.

Place this jar in a larger one or in a large glass bowl. When the frog quiets down, look at its throat. The throat moves up and down regularly as it breathes.

Begin adding ice and salt to the outside container. This mixture causes a drop in temperature of the water inside the smaller jar. As this water gets colder, the frog's throat moves more slowly. When the water is about 32°F (0°C), the frog closes its eyes and expels the air from its lungs. It begins to make digging movements with its legs as if it were making a hole in the mud. Then it stops. It stretches out and just lies there. It looks almost dead.

The frog can be removed from the jar at this time. It will feel stiff and cold. It should be handled for no more than a few minutes, then quickly replaced. The warm hands can revive it, and it may jump away. A little warm water may be added to the frog's water. The frog comes out of hibernation very quickly. It sits up, and its throat begins to move up and down. The frog behaves as if winter had just gone and spring had arrived.

There are many more cold-blooded hibernators, for example, wasps, spiders, fish, and snakes. Each has its special time and place for hibernating. Each goes into a long, deathlike sleep for the same reason—to survive the winter.

THE SEVEN SLEEPERS

Seven famous animals live in the Northeast part of the United States. They are famous for a very strange reason: All take long winter naps. The Seven Sleepers are the:

1. Woodchuck
2. Little brown bat
3. Jumping mouse
4. Bear
5. Chipmunk
6. Skunk and
7. Raccoon.

They are all mammals. Mammals are alike in several ways. They are warm-blooded. They give birth to babies that are nursed with their mother's milk. Their bodies are covered with hair or fur. In most other ways, all mammals are quite different from each other. Each of the Seven Sleepers has a most interesting life story.

The Woodchuck

The woodchuck is the most famous of the Seven Sleepers. Almost everyone knows that it is a true hibernator because people are so interested in the legend of Ground Hog Day. (Ground hog is another name for woodchuck.)

According to this story, the ground hog awakens from hibernation on the second day of February. It comes up from its burrow to have a look around. If the day is bright and sunny, it sees its shadow. This frightens the animal so much that it dashes back underground, where it will remain six more weeks. This is a sign that the weather will remain cold and that it will be six weeks before spring.

But February second may be a dull, cloudy day. Then, according to the story, the ground hog does not see its shadow. Therefore, it is not frightened and does not return to its burrow. People believe that this means that winter is over and that it will be mild from that day on.

It is best not to depend upon a woodchuck to predict the weather. The truth is that whether or not the sun shines on February second, spring is about six weeks away.

It is true that woodchucks do appear aboveground at about this time, but not to predict the weather. This is their breeding time. Only the males leave their burrows. They are interested in finding mates.

Mating may take place late in January, February, or, sometimes, March. It depends upon where the woodchuck lives. Woodchucks usually mate in the female's burrow. If the weather is mild, and there is food around, the male may remain aboveground.

However, it is usually cold and wintry outdoors. Snow may still cover the ground, and food is probably scarce. Most often the woodchuck retires to his burrow to continue his winter nap. Several weeks later, his brain will notify the rest of his body that it is time to awaken. By then winter is over, spring has arrived, grasses and clover are growing in the meadows. The ground hog will come to the surface once more and start dining. Besides feeding on plants, it may also eat some small animals. Woodchucks may feed on snails, insects, and other small creatures. However, they are chiefly plant eaters.

Woodchucks are familiar animals. They are active during the day when people are about. Frequently, these animals are seen feeding by the roadside or dashing across the road. Unfortunately, they do not always reach the other side. Many dead woodchucks are found on the highways.

The woodchuck is a chunky animal with a short, bushy tail. An adult may weigh as much as 10 pounds (4½ kilograms). It stands about 2 feet (over half a meter) tall. Its thick, coarse fur is usually a grizzled brown color. It has four short, dark, powerful legs with black feet. The sharp claws are used for digging. Some woodchucks have very light fur, and others are almost black.

The woodchuck has a curious habit of suddenly popping up very straight. It sniffs the air and looks around with its sharp eyes to check if everything is safe. Woodchucks fear foxes, dogs, hawks, and people. If a woodchuck senses danger, it plunges right down into one of its holes. The hole leads into its tunnel. The animal seldom strays very far from one of the entrances to its burrow.

The woodchuck lives in woods near open fields or along fence rows. Its summer den is built in a meadow where there is a good food supply. Usually its winter quarters are dug near the edge of a field where there are trees and shrubs. Snow that collects among the woody stems of these plants acts as a warm blanket above the den.

The main entrance to the woodchuck's tunnel is usually beneath a rock or a tree stump. The woodchuck removes a great deal of soil and many stones in digging its tunnel. These it piles up outside the main entrance. The top of this little pile makes a handy lookout post for the animal. It is also used for sunbathing and as a toilet. After the animal drops some waste there, it covers it up with fresh soil.

The tunnel slopes down for 4 to 5 feet (1 to 1½ meters). Animals always dig winter tunnels below the frost line. Woodchucks have to do a great deal of digging. The tunnel may be 40 feet (12 meters) long and have, in addition, several entrances. The chambers are used as nests. The main nest is the largest. It may be 12 inches (30 centimeters) high and 18 inches (about 45 centimeters) wide. The nests are placed high in the burrow so that water will not flood them. The woodchucks line them with leaves and grasses—the same kinds of materials that other animals use. The animal sleeps and cares for its young in its burrow, which is also a place of safety.

Most of the woodchuck's springtime and summertime activity is eating. It eats more and more and gets fatter and fatter. It feeds in the morning and again in the afternoon. It takes time out for sunbathing and napping. Napping is usually done in the burrow, where it feels safest.

Woody eats more and sleeps less toward the end of summer. He grows so fat that he can barely walk.

At last the woodchuck stops eating, even though there is plenty of green food all around. It seems to have lost its appetite. It stays in its burrow more and more. It comes out of its burrow several times just to empty its bowels. All true hibernators cleanse themselves this way. Then they are ready to turn in for their long winter sleep.

When the woodchuck is finally ready to go into hibernation, it plugs up the entrance to its burrow. It does this from the inside by pushing soil against the hole. This keeps out the cold as well as enemies. The upper part of the burrow remains open. It is often used by foxes, skunks, or rabbits during the winter.

After Woody closes the opening, he goes into his bedroom. His heart and other body parts work more and more slowly. Little by little, as his body gets colder, he rolls himself into a ball and finally sinks into a deep sleep. This long winter nap may last for six months.

During hibernation the woodchuck's heart beats four times a minute instead of eighty. Instead of breathing twenty-five times a minute, it now takes one breath in five minutes. The body temperature of about 100°F (38°C) drops to 37°F (2.7°C). This is just a few degrees above freezing.

The woodchuck remains in this state all winter. It can survive the most severe weather because its den will not drop below freezing. If Woody should get too cold, he begins to shiver and awaken somewhat. His body warms up, and he continues to hibernate without freezing to death.

In the spring the woodchuck's body clock signals for the season's awakening. This time it feels the urge to get up and out. It takes a shorter time to come out of hibernation than to go into it. The woodchuck starts to breathe more quickly. This sends more oxygen into the blood. The heart beats faster. It may even jump to two hundred beats a minute, causing the blood to circulate faster. The fat layer under its fur begins to break down and supplies the animal with much energy.

The woodchuck starts to shiver. The body warms up. In a few hours Woody has awakened from his long winter nap. A very skinny Woody comes above the ground for a breath of fresh air. Now he weighs only half what he did before hibernation; but when he looks around with a good meal in mind, there is plenty to eat.

Baby woodchucks arrive in April or May. A litter may consist of four or five young ones. Their eyes are closed, and they are quite helpless. They remain in their mother's nest for several weeks. Although she goes out to eat, she returns regularly to nurse the babies and to take care of them.

After about a month, the infants open their eyes. Then

they are ready to explore their world. Soon they find the opening of the burrow. They go out, never to return. Each one builds a shallow burrow of its own near the old one. This collection of burrows forms a kind of nursery. Mother is still around, and she continues to look after them.

After a few weeks, the young leave for good. First each one searches for a proper place to dig a new tunnel. It must be near a food supply of tender green plants.

Once the home is completed, the young animals are ready to carry on the yearly program of the woodchuck, which includes a great deal of eating. The animal must be well fed in order to hibernate at the end of the warm season.

The Little Brown Bat

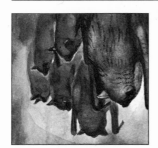

Bats are the only mammals that can fly. One of the commonest is the little brown bat. It has long, brownish, silky fur. Its sharp little eyes and pointed ears may remind one of a mouse. In fact, its scientific name, *Myotis*, comes from two Greek words that mean "mouse ear."

Its front legs look like hands with long, thin, bony fingers. Its hind legs are short. Each has five tiny, hooked claws. The finger bones, the hind feet, and the tail are all connected by a thin web. This web of elastic skin forms the bat's wing. Although the little brown bat may be only 3½ inches (about 9 centimeters) long, its wings can spread to almost 10 inches (25 centimeters).

The bat has two little thumb hooks on the upper sides of the wing. It uses these for pulling itself along the ground or for scratching. The claws on the hind legs are not covered by the wing. These are used for holding on when it hangs. Bats hang upside down.

Bats are excellent fliers. They fly mostly at night. However, they are able to see by day as well as by night. Even if they are blindfolded, bats know just where to fly. They have a kind of built-in sonar system that works somewhat like sonar instruments on submarines.

A bat continues to give off signals while it is flying. Some of these sound like squeaks to the human ear, but we can't hear most of them because the pitch is too high. The signals strike objects around the bat. Echoes bounce back from the objects to the animal's ears. These echoes tell the bat where an object is located as well as its size and shape.

All this information travels so quickly to the bat that it can decide immediately where to go. It may make a quick turn in order not to hit something. Or it may head straight for the object because it is a gnat or a mosquito. A bat can receive a returning echo from an insect, then swoop down and catch it in less than one second.

Bats feed chiefly at dusk and at dawn. They may rest during the night, in between periods of feeding. By the time the sun rises, however, the bats usually retire for the day. They seek a quiet, dark spot for their daily sleeping period. Some of their favorite hiding places are inside unused attics, barns, tree hollows, church towers, chimneys, or under the loose bark of trees.

The best time to see the little brown bat is in the spring and summer as the sun is setting. As long as it remains light, they can be seen flying this way and that as they avoid some objects and gobble up flying insects. When they fly over water, they often swoop down for a drink.

By the time summer ends, the bat has become quite fat. It may weigh about one-fourth of an ounce (7 grams) early in the spring. By the end of summer, it may weigh three times as much. The added weight is extra fat. The bat is getting ready to hibernate. The weather is turning colder, and soon flying insects will be scarce.

Some little brown bats hibernate in caves. They collect in large colonies inside where it is not too dry and the temperature is above freezing. The conditions in the cave remain the same all winter.

Other little brown bats hibernate in some of the same places where they take their daily naps during the warm weather. Hibernating bats have been found in places such as tree hollows, old buildings, and under the eaves of roofs. They winter in such places by themselves or in very small groups.

The little brown bats go into hibernation very quickly. They hang themselves up by their little claws. Their body temperature drops down rapidly to a few degrees above the temperature of the air around them. Their blood moves very slowly as their heart beats slower. They breathe only about once every minute. They just hang for three to four months. By the time it has warmed up and insects are flying once more, their brains signal them to awaken. They come out of hibernation quickly and get to work at once.

The little brown bats mate before they hibernate. When the hibernating period is over, the females are the first to revive. Those that are pregnant form nursery colonies. They usually leave the caves they hibernated in and gather somewhere else. They choose a place where they will spend the rest of spring and summer. The females whose babies are born go to the same spot. Those who are still pregnant go to another. Males usually go off by themselves.

A bat gives birth to one baby. Bat babies are quite large. An infant may weigh a third of its mother's weight. If a human baby weighed a third of its mother's weight at birth, it could easily weigh 40 pounds (18 kilograms).

The little brown bat mother holds the baby in her wing while the infant nurses at her breast. When mother bat gets hungry, she flies about catching insects while baby holds onto her neck. The infant grows rapidly. At times it gets too heavy for the flying mother. She then hangs the baby up on a twig while she catches her food. When the little one is a month old, it is able to fly by itself.

Many strange things are said about bats. People think that they get into your hair, that bats carry bedbugs, that they are dirty, that they are blind, that they are a sign of bad luck. None of these stories is true.

The Chinese have a better idea. In their culture, bats are considered to be a good sign, a sign of happiness.

The Jumping Mouse

 You might imagine that an animal called a jumping mouse is both small and a good jumper. Perhaps you have a pet gerbil, a distant cousin to the jumping mouse. The gerbil is sometimes called a "pocket kangaroo" because it is so small and, like the jumping mouse, can leap so well with its strong hind legs. The jumping mouse weighs less than an ounce (only 20 grams). Its body may measure only 3 inches (7½ centimeters) in length, but it has a long tail, longer than its body. It also has very long hind legs and feet that are developed for jumping. The animal looks like a very small kangaroo. When it jumps through the grass, it resembles a leaping frog.

Jumping mice can leap a distance of 10 feet (3 meters). The long tail helps to balance the mouse as it goes through the air. If, by accident, one loses its tail, it also loses its balance. Then, instead of sailing straight through the air, it usually somersaults and falls to the ground.

The jumping mouse has an attractive, two-toned fur

coat that is yellowish brown on top and lighter yellowish orange on the sides. There is little fur on the tail.

Like the little brown bat, these mice are true hibernators. They usually go into their long, deep sleep by the end of October. They start putting on weight in September. They need to put on a certain amount of fat before they get the urge to hibernate. If an animal has eaten enough to put on the necessary amount of fat sooner, it hibernates sooner.

Before it hibernates, the jumping mouse builds a special hibernating tunnel. It digs way down below the frost line and at the end of its tunnel it prepares a nest. When the animal is ready to go below for the season, it starts to rearrange things in the tunnel. First it plugs up the entrance hole from inside. Then it moves its nest next to the entrance.

Its body then goes through the same kinds of changes that take place in other hibernating mammals. It gets cold as its body temperature falls. Its breathing rate and heart rate slow down. Blood moves through the body more slowly. The little mouse buries its head between its hind legs and winds its long tail around its body. Like the others, it resembles a fur ball, but a very small one.

The little round shape exists that way for about seven months. It shrinks as its layer of fat is used up to keep it alive. Of course, it needs very little energy during hibernation.

The jumping mouse has its spring awakening sometime in late April or May. Males come out first. Females follow in a few weeks. First the animals seek food, for they are hungry after such a long fast. Then they search for a mate.

Eighteen days after mating, six tiny mice are born. One female may give birth to three litters a year. She may have eighteen children in one season.

It is hard to imagine an infant that weighs only one twenty-eighth of an ounce (about one gram—there are approximately 28 grams in an ounce). It is tiny, naked, and helpless. Mouse mothers nurse and look after their babies as mammal mothers do. The babies grow up quickly. By the end of a week, they have some dark fur on their bodies. By the time they are four or five weeks old, they leave home. Some of them even have families of their own that very same year.

As soon as a young jumping mouse leaves its mother, it builds a home of its own. It makes a summer nest of grass and leaves in a shallow burrow. Sometimes the nest is placed in a hollow log or even in a little mound of grass. This place is used for protection and for sleeping.

The summer is spent in eating and in raising families. These mice must also be on the lookout for enemies. Jumping mice live in meadows, hayfields, grain fields, or woodlands. There are many predators in such areas. Hawks and foxes are among the animals that feed on jumping mice. The long leaps that jumping mice can make often save their lives. But as hibernation time gets closer, the mice get fatter, and a fat jumping mouse cannot jump as far or as fast as a thinner one. This is too bad, for the very same fat that helps a jumping mouse to survive the cold winter may be responsible for an early autumn death.

The Bear

Smokey the Bear, now famous, was a black bear rescued from a forest fire when he was very young, just a cub. Bears are forest animals.

The black bear is the most common bear in North America. It has a thick fur coat the color of which varies according to where it lives, although the face is always brown. Since it was first discovered in the East, where the animal's fur is black, it was named "black bear." Out West and in the Northwest, these bears usually have a brown fur coat. There they are called cinnamon bears. Still other bears have gray fur. All these bears are alike—the only difference is the color of the fur.

Bears are not true hibernators. They usually sleep through the worst weather, but their body temperature never drops very low while they sleep. A bear can easily be aroused from its winter sleep by a loud noise or a bright light.

Bears are big eaters, but before winter arrives they eat even more than usual. They eat just about anything they can find—berries, fruit, nuts, mice, insects, honey, grass, and dead animals. The bears get very fat. The fat under their fur coats may grow 4 inches (over 10 centimeters) thick. When there is plenty of food around, the bears may keep on eating. They may not turn in for their long sleep until the middle of winter. If food is scarce, they may take a long nap much earlier. This sometimes happens when there is an early snowfall.

The snow may cover all roots, berries, and other foods. Then the bears' brains send out signals that it is sleeping time. If the weather should turn mild again, they awaken and search for food. Then they go back to sleep.

Bears look for sheltered spots in which to take their long winter naps. A bear may choose a hollow tree or a shallow cave, or even a space in a rock pile. Sometimes bears dig their own winter dens in the ground. The female is much fussier than the male. She searches for a very snug den because that is where her babies will be born.

Mother bear usually gives birth to twin babies. She cleans them, nurses them, and takes very good care of them. The infant cubs are very small. They are about 8 inches (20 centimeters) long. They weigh 2 pounds (less than a kilogram). The mother may weigh as much as 300 pounds (136 kilograms). The new babies are naked and must be kept very warm. Their eyes remain closed for about four weeks. When the cubs are two months old, they can follow their mother about.

By that time, it is spring. Mother and babies come out of their dens. They are hungry, thirsty, and raring to go.

First, they search for water. Bears drink a great deal of water right after their long winter naps. Then they search for food.

There is much for the cubs to learn, and their mother

is an excellent teacher. The cubs must know what to eat and how to get certain foods. Their mother teaches them how to turn over a log for ants, how to get honey from a beehive, how to catch a mouse or a fish.

Bears do most of their eating at dusk, and they can often be seen around garbage dumps of hotels and campsites then.

The mother does not allow anybody to go near her cubs, not even the father. If she senses danger, she pushes the young up a tree. They are good climbers.

Bears have very poor eyesight, but they can hear very well. They also have a good sense of smell. If they hear a strange sound, they may stand up and smell the air to discover if there is any danger. They are shy animals and usually run away when they are frightened. But a mother always fights to protect her cubs.

Bears also become aggressive when they smell food. Sometimes they hurt people who try to offer them food. It is always unwise to feed bears.

The cubs remain with their mother all through the spring and summer. They den up with her the following winter until it is summertime once more. Then they go off on their own. Mother bear is busy preparing for her next set of twins. Bears have babies every other year.

Besides the black bear group, there is the Alaskan brown bear. This bear lives along the bays and rivers of the Pacific coast. Some of these bears weigh as much as 1,500 pounds (680 kilograms). They are grazers, feeding on a grasslike plant that grows in wet areas. They also eat small animals, such as mice.

When the time comes for their winter sleep, they den

up in a hilly area. There the land is dry. The mothers have two or three babies during this time. These bears usually leave their dens in April, even though there may still be snow on the ground.

In the spring, the Alaskan brown bears catch the salmon that come up the rivers and streams in order to spawn. They most often catch the dying salmon, the ones that have completed their spawning. However, many salmon fishermen shoot the bears because they believe the bears are stealing their fish.

The grizzly bear is the bear that sportsmen enjoy so much. They claim that it is the most dangerous game to shoot. Unfortunately, it has been so widely hunted that it is now in danger of becoming extinct. There are a few left in the North and in the Northwest.

Most people think that the grizzly is the largest of the bears, but it is only about half the size of the Alaskan brown bear. Before Europeans came to North America, the grizzly had no fear of humans. However, it now has become very fearful of their guns.

A male grizzly bear may weigh from 400 to 1,000 pounds (180 to 450 kilograms). It is a very strong animal. It has sharp, curved claws on its front feet. The silver tips on its dark fur give it a grayish or grizzled appearance, and this is how it got the name *grizzly*.

Grizzlies will eat plant foods such as leaves, grasses, and fruits. However, they are very good hunters, and they seem to prefer meat. At times they have killed and eaten cattle.

Grizzlies take long winter naps as most other bears do. During this period, one to four helpless babies are born to a female. The grizzly mother is very dangerous if anyone comes near her babies. However, normally if there is any fear of being hurt, the grizzlies prefer to run away. They are fast runners. A grizzly can run even faster than a horse for a short distance.

The polar bear is an arctic animal of the frozen north. Its world is made up of ice and snow. It wears a coat that matches its background, for it is snow white and very thick.

The polar bear is different from the other three kinds of bears. Although it has a small head for its size, it is the largest bear of all.

It roams the icy land and waters all year long. It is a meat eater and a good hunter. It goes after seals, walruses, and the mouselike lemmings. Sometimes it nibbles on low-growing plants such as mosses and lichens.

Only the female polar bear takes long winter naps. She does so when she is pregnant or when she still has young cubs to bring up. At such times she leaves the edge of the ice near the water and goes inland. There she dens up for the winter.

Hunters go after polar bears in airplanes. They chase the bears, then shoot them with powerful rifles. Although polar bears are excellent hunters and fighters, they cannot run fast enough to escape these rifles. Each year there are fewer of these beautiful wild animals left on this earth.

The Chipmunk

 A chipmunk is full of energy. It is fun to watch one scamper through open woods, over boulders, and along stone fences. A chipmunk is only about 8 inches (20 centimeters) long, and about half of that is tail. It has brown fur with yellowish orange and black stripes down its back. It looks and acts like an animated toy.

Some people believe that the position in which the chipmunk holds its tail can forecast the winter weather. They say that when a chippy runs with its tail straight out, the winter will be mild. When the tail is held straight up, it will be a colder winter. If it lies down along Chippy's back, then one may expect very severe weather. There is no proof that this is so.

Chipmunks are bright eyed and very alert. They have a sharp sense of smell, and they also see and hear very well.

Chippies are among the friendliest wild mammals. They can barely resist peanuts. If you offer some to a chipmunk, it will shortly become your good friend. It will take peanuts from your hand, your hat, or your pocket. Sometimes it opens the peanut and eats it at once. At other times it grabs the peanut and stuffs it into its cheeks. Then it rushes to its underground home where it stores away the nut. Chipmunks have very elastic cheek pouches that can stretch to hold a great deal of food at a time.

The chipmunk's habit of storing food is how it got part of its scientific name. Scientists call it *Tamius striatus. Tamius* comes from a Greek word that means "a storer." The *striatus* part is from the Latin and means "striped." The chipmunk's common name came from the Algonquian Indians. They called it *chitmunk*. It usually makes a *chip chip chip* sound. Some people say that there are times when a chippy sings almost like a bird.

The striped storer does spend a good deal of its time storing food. Toward the end of summer, it speeds up this activity. Chippy collects nuts, acorns, and grains, which it packs away in its burrow. Before it retires for a long winter nap, it may have harvested almost half a bushel (18 liters) of food.

Chipmunks keep most of this food in special storage chambers that they build in their burrows. A good supply of food is also placed under the bed. This bed is made of dried leaves and grasses and is very soft. Chippy spends most of the winter in bed, so this is a very handy arrangement. Whenever it feels hungry, it just reaches down and nibbles away. By the time winter is over, the food is gone, and the bed is on the floor.

Chipmunks may be seen running about as late as November. When the temperature drops down toward freezing, the animal gets an urge to take a winter nap. Its body begins to work more slowly. It has no extra body fat to supply energy during the winter. Instead of storing fat under its skin, the chipmunk stores food under its bed and in its storerooms. It is well provided for in the cold weather.

The animal awakens several times during the winter. It has some dinner and goes back to sleep. If it is mild and sunny, the chipmunk may go out for a scamper, a sun-bath, or a drink of snow. With the arrival of another cold spell, it retires to its cozy den for another long nap.

By late February or early March, a chipmunk's brain sends the rest of its body a message. It feels that this is the time to get up and out. Males are usually the first to leave their burrows. They eat and drink. Then they go forth to search for a mate.

A month after mating, four or five tiny, helpless babies are born. Another set may be born in July. The babies remain in the snug, dark nest below for about three months. Fur grows in when they are about a week old. Their eyes open at age four weeks. Mother is up and out all this time, but she comes down regularly to nurse them and to care for them.

The babies grow up quickly. In a few weeks they begin to chase each other through the tunnel. They discover the store of food and learn how to eat it. They use their sharp little teeth to get to the meat of nuts and acorns. At the age of three months, the young find their way out of the burrow. Then they explore their world and find their own food.

Although they can climb trees, they usually remain on the ground. They discover the good taste of fresh fruits and berries. They also eat some fresh flowers. They include some animal foods as well. They eat insects, earthworms, and baby mice. Sometimes they visit a bird's nest. There they might dine on an unhatched egg or possibly on a baby bird.

Soon it is time to lead their own lives and they leave home. This means that each chipmunk must dig a new burrow. They choose just the right spot. It must have loose soil, and it has to be in a safe place. They make the entrance to the burrow under roots, logs, or rocks. Sometimes a chipmunk makes its den in a hollow log or in a stump. It may even dig its home under somebody's cabin in the woods.

The burrow consists of a very long, twisted tunnel. A chipmunk uses its nose and paws as it digs. First it digs straight down for about 12 inches (30 centimeters). Then it continues downward on a slope for about 5 feet (1½ meters). This brings the tunnel below the freezing line. The tunnel then continues for another 30 feet (9 meters). It has many twists and turns. The burrow is about 2 inches (5 centimeters) wide, but there are many side chambers or rooms that are larger.

The central chamber is a bedroom. This is about 12 by 12 inches (30 by 30 centimeters). Here is where Chippy sleeps. The babies are also born in this room. The other rooms are smaller. They are used for storing the winter food supply.

Chippy is a clean animal, and the room at the very bottom is used only as a toilet.

When the burrow is finished, the chipmunk plugs up the original hole. It scatters the soil that it had brought up from below. Then it covers the spot with leaves and grass. This disguises the old entrance. Then the chipmunk makes one or more new, well-hidden entrance holes.

The chipmunk is excellently fitted to winter in the Northeast. It does not hibernate straight through the cold season as does the little brown bat. However, at times it is just as inactive. It does not have much stored body fat to depend upon as the other sleepers do. It is the only one of the Seven Sleepers that stores winter food instead of body fat.

The Skunk

Skunks are woodland animals that frequently live near towns. You can often see them prowling around garbage cans at dusk. Woodsmen know them as "wood pussies." There are several kinds of skunks. The striped skunk, which is about the size of a house cat, is most common.

The skunk's body is stout. It has a small head with small eyes and short ears. It also has short legs, but its tail is long, bushy, and beautiful.

Most of its fur is black and shiny. There is a thin white stripe down the front of its face. More white decorates the back of its head. There are two stripes of white along its back. The black and white fur designs are not exactly the same on all the animals. Each skunk has a slightly different pattern.

A skunk can dig a hole and call it home. Sometimes the hole is under a cabin. It may be in a hollow tree or in an old log. It may even be a home once used by a fox or a woodchuck. It always makes a nest of dry leaves and grasses at the end of the den.

Although the skunk is active all night, it sometimes leaves its den in the afternoon to search for food. Its usual time to get going is at dusk. It eats both plant and animal foods, such as insects, mice, moles, shrews, rats, or berries.

The skunk walks with dignity. It steps along slowly with its fine tail slightly raised. There are two scent glands at the base of the tail. If the animal is frightened, its tail goes up even higher. This is a warning. Sometimes it stamps its feet and chatters as an additional warning. If this does not scare off an enemy, the skunk quickly turns its back to it. Then the skunk discharges a very smelly, oily liquid from its scent glands. This brings results—the enemy flees. The skunk has an accurate aim for up to 12 feet (3½ meters).

The skunk is one of the lightest nappers among the Seven Sleepers. It gets ready for winter in late summer. It digs a deeper den, down below the frost line. It builds up a very large, soft nest inside of it. The winter bed may be made up of as much as a bushel (35 liters) of dry leaves and grasses. The skunk eats a great deal, and, of course, it puts on weight.

As the weather gets colder, the skunk spends more time in bed. If the winter happens to be mild, it remains active much longer. When the thermometer drops below 50°F (10°C), the young skunks get very drowsy. They retire first. When it gets even colder, the females join them. When there is a real freeze, the males turn in for a nap.

The body temperature of skunks does not drop very low as it does in the true hibernators. Skunks' temperatures remain high during their winter sleep. They also keep warm by huddling together in a community den. The rest of the year they live by themselves.

The end of winter is breeding time for the skunk. The male, if it was sleeping, comes out first. The female remains in the den a little longer. When a male finds a female, they mate. Nine weeks later, a litter of four babies arrives. By then it is spring.

Each little one weighs only about a half ounce (15 grams). It is wrinkled and naked, but the black and white color pattern of its fur can be seen. The young leave the burrow just as soon as they can walk. For a while they stay close to Mother. They walk in a single file behind her. This is a charming sight that can often be seen in the woods. Sometimes such a parade of skunks takes place at the edge of a town, where it stops traffic.

Mother skunk looks after her family all spring, summer, and winter. After the young come out of their winter den, they are one year old and ready to seek their fortunes. Each finds a summer home of its own or builds a new one.

Skunks are attractive and fascinating animals. They are to be admired for their appearance and observed for their habits—but from a distance. It is most difficult to get rid of skunk smell. People who live in the suburbs know how important it is to have tight covers on their garbage pails. Light sleepers, such as raccoons and skunks, can become all-year visitors wherever food is available.

The Raccoon

The raccoon is an animal that is most active at night, although sometimes it can be seen during the day. Its long, thick fur is a mixture of gray, black, and brown. The bushy tail is very handsome with rings of black and gray. Early pioneers decorated their hats with raccoon tails.

The raccoon has a black mask across its face and eyes. Sometimes the raccoon is called the masked bandit, not only because it looks like one, but also because it manages to get into cabins and farm houses. It opens cans and boxes and makes off with cookies, sugar, and other goodies.

Raccoons are found where there are trees near water. A raccoon often makes its home in a tree hollow, among some rocks, or in an old squirrel's nest. Sometimes it moves into an unused woodchuck burrow. It may even have several dens at once.

The raccoon eats many things, but it prefers animal food. It digs for earthworms and insect larvae in the ground. Larvae are undeveloped insects. It also catches adult insects, mice, and frogs. Along the waterways it goes after fish, crayfish, and other shellfish. Berries, sweet corn, melon, and grapes are some of the plant foods that it eats. Sometimes it washes its food before eating it. It does not do this each time, as some people believe.

The raccoon has five toes with sharp little claws on each foot. They look somewhat like the hands and feet of a human baby. These claws are used to get at food and to climb trees. The name *raccoon* comes from the Indian word *arakun*, which means "he scratches with his hands."

Autumn is feasting time for the raccoon. It eats and eats, and most of its food turns into fat. This is the time of year when the "masked bandit" raids farmers' gardens. When the weather starts turning cold, the raccoon may decide to take a good nap.

The raccoon is a very light sleeper. Like the bear's, its body temperature and heart rate remain high all winter. Sometimes the raccoon just sleeps out a big winter storm. At other times it may den up for a few weeks.

An adult usually lives by itself during the warm seasons. However, several animals may share a winter den. After a storm, a number of trails can be found on the snow. Raccoons go abroad searching for food and for unfrozen water. Raccoons that live in the South do not take any long winter naps.

By the end of January, the animals begin to search for mates no matter how cold it may be. However, if it is below 20°F (-6.5°C), the raccoons usually return to their dens until February.

The females have their babies in the spring. The infants are born with fur, but their eyes remain closed for the first few weeks. The mothers look after the young, which are called kits. For the first two months, the mother raccoons nurse the kits with milk from their bodies.

The kits remain with their mothers until the following spring. Then they go house-hunting. They look for vacant tree hollows or suitable caves in which to make a den. Each one begins to carry on an active raccoon life of its own.

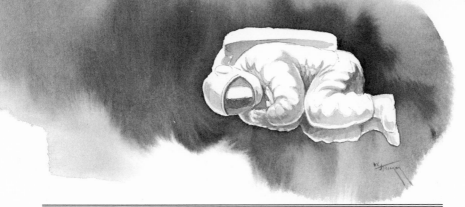

CAN HUMAN BEINGS HIBERNATE?

People have always learned from other animals. There was a time, many thousands of years ago, when people first began to wear clothing made of fur and wool. They imitated such creatures as wolves and sheep. Such clothing helped people of long ago to survive cold winters. People today still wear wool and fur.

More recently, people have observed that some animals survive winter weather by moving away. They migrate south each fall and return north in the spring. With more and better transportation, people also migrate. They can use ships, trains, automobiles, and airplanes to take them from cold climates to where it is warmer.

Now scientists are investigating the hibernation of animals. Perhaps they can learn something about this process that can help people. Scientists are interested in several things about true hibernators.

Their bodies get close to freezing during hibernation. They do not easily feel pain. Their body functions become very slow. They do not bleed if cut. They are not easily hurt by poison gas. They need very little energy while they are sleeping. There is no need for food or drink.

Doctors realize how useful it would be to operate on very cold bodies. There would be no pain and no bleeding. Certain kinds of surgery could be carried out more safely.

Until recently, surgeons were unable to perform some special, delicate operations. These can now be done, for doctors have developed a way to make the body very cold. The patient is packed in ice. The body temperature gets very low. There is practically no action of the heart, lungs, or kidneys. The body is alive, but it is working very slowly. After the operation, the patient is gradually warmed and returns to normal. Many lives have been saved as a result.

This kind of freezing is different from hibernation. However, the scientists learned much about this new technique from studying hibernating animals.

Scientists imagine that there would be many benefits to be gained if people could really hibernate.

Suppose there were a plane crash in the frozen north. If the passengers could go into hibernation until they were rescued, they would not be in danger of death.

Hibernation could also be useful in space travel. Much less food and oxygen would be needed for long trips. Storage room is a very big problem in spaceships.

If astronauts could curl up and go to sleep for several months on very long space flights, they would not get bored. This would make space flight easier for many passengers.

However, people cannot hibernate—yet. Perhaps someday they will. The study of hibernation continues. Many new discoveries about this process will probably be made in the future.

Right now, we know that whether animals are true hibernators, like the

    woodchuck,

    little brown bat, and

    jumping mouse,

or whether they are just snoozers, like the

    bear,

    chipmunk,

    skunk, and

    raccoon,

people are learning a great deal from studying the interesting lives of such animals as the Seven Sleepers.

INDEX